THE FROG PRINCESS

August 1984

To our Snail Princess
with lots of love,

Myron and Lyndeann

THE FROG PRINCESS

Retold by Elizabeth Isele

Illustrated by Michael Hague

THOMAS Y. CROWELL

New York

Adapted from a tale
originally collected and recorded
by the Russian folklorist
Aleksandr Afanasiev (1826–1871).

The Frog Princess
Text copyright © 1984 by Elizabeth Isele
Illustrations copyright © 1984 by Michael Hague

Thomas Y. Crowell Junior Books, 10 East 53rd Street,
New York, NY. 10022. Published simultaneously in
Canada by Fitzhenry & Whiteside Limited, Toronto.
Designed by Harriet Barton
10 9 8 7 6 5 4 3 2 1
First Edition

Library of Congress Cataloging in Publication Data
Isele, Elizabeth.
 The frog princess.

 Adaptation of: Tŝarevna-liagushka.
 Summary: Forced to marry an ugly frog, the youngest
son of the Czar is astounded to learn that the frog is
really the beautiful princess Vasilisa the Wise.
 [1. Folklore—Soviet Union. 2. Fairy tales] 1. Hague,
Michael, ill. II. Tŝarevna-liagushka. III. Title.
PZ8.1.I725Fr 1984   398.2452787'0947 [E]   81-43883
ISBN 0-690-04217-5
ISBN 0-690-04218-3 (lib. bdg.)

*For Karlin, Jordan, Erinn, Lauren,
and our extended family*

E.I.

For Sue

M.H.

Long ago in Russia there lived a Czar who had three fine sons. When they grew old enough to marry, the Czar called the three princes before him and said:

"My sons, each of you must take his strongest bow and one arrow. Go beyond the palace walls, to the field where no one is permitted to hunt. There you will draw your bow tight and shoot far into the sky. Whoever picks up your arrow will be your bride."

The first prince's arrow fell in a nobleman's courtyard, where it was picked up by his daughter. The second one's arrow landed by a general's house and was picked up by his daughter. But the youngest prince, Ivan, had shot his arrow so far it could not be seen at all.

For two days Ivan searched in vain for it. But then, on the third day, in the middle of a swamp he found an ugly frog with his arrow in her mouth. As he bent to take the arrow, the frog spoke out. "You may have your arrow," she said, "if you take me for your wife."

Startled to hear the frog speak, Ivan slowly bent down to pick up the creature. She gave him the arrow, and he placed her carefully in his pocket to carry her back to the palace.

When Ivan arrived at the palace with his arrow and a frog in his pocket, his brothers and their brides-to-be laughed at him. Weeping, Ivan told his story to the Czar.

"How can I marry a frog?" he said. "Certainly this loathsome, croaking marsh creature is not worthy of being the wife of a prince!"

"If the fates would have you marry a frog, you must," said the Czar. "You cannot go against fate."

And the three weddings took place the very next day. While there was joy in the hearts of his brothers and their brides, there was none for Ivan. He arrived in a closed carriage, and he carried his frog bride on a golden plate. (Unhappy as he was, Ivan treated his bride with kindness.)

Not long after the weddings the Czar again summoned his three sons. He commanded that their wives make him gifts so he could see how skillful each one was. "Take some linen from my storeroom," he said, "and ask your wives to make me a shirt by morning."

The wives of the two older sons were not at all worried. They knew they could sew well, but they laughed to think of what the little frog might do.

Ivan went home with his head hung down in sadness. "How could my wife make a shirt?" he thought. "She who knows only how to creep and croak."

"Kwa, kwa," said the frog when she saw Ivan. "What has made you so sad?"

"The Czar," moaned Ivan, "has ordered you to make a fine linen shirt for him by morning."

"Fear not," said the frog. "Go to bed and rest, for the morning brings more wisdom than the evening."

As soon as the prince fell asleep, the bride hopped out of her frog skin. This was not a frog at all, but rather Vasilisa the Wise, a beautiful princess. She stepped to the window and threw the linen out upon the winds.

"Come, my maidens," she called. "Take this cloth and make a shirt as fine as one my own father would wear."

Before morning the maidens returned with a beautiful shirt. The princess placed the shirt beside the bed of the sleeping prince and stepped back into her frog skin before he awoke.

When he opened his eyes and saw the shirt, the prince was overjoyed. At once he set out for the palace, where his brothers were already presenting their shirts to the Czar.

When the first son placed his shirt before his father, the Czar shouted in disgust, "This shirt is not fit for a peasant!" When he saw the second shirt, the Czar said he would only wear that to his bath. But the Czar's eyes shone when he saw Ivan's shirt embroidered in gold and silver. He exclaimed, "This shirt is fit for a Czar to wear on the grandest holidays!"

Grumbling, the brothers set out for home. "Maybe we were wrong about our brother's bride," they said. "Perhaps she's not a frog at all, but a cunning witch!"

It was not long before the Czar summoned his sons again. This time he said, "Each of you take enough flour and sugar from my storehouse to show me which of your wives can bake the finest cake by morning."

Now an even sorrier Ivan returned to his frog bride.

"Kwa, kwa," croaked the frog. "Why are you so sad, Ivan?"

"How could I not be sad, Little Croaker? My father has commanded you to bake him a fine white cake by morning."

"Your sadness is for nothing," said the frog. "Go to bed and rest, Ivan. The morning brings more wisdom than the evening."

Not to be outdone a second time, the brides of the two elder sons sent a young maid to spy on the frog to see how she would make her cake. But the clever frog guessed what they were doing, so she mixed some dough and threw it directly onto some hot flat stones in the fire. The spying girl rushed away to report to her mistresses how they must bake their cakes.

Meanwhile the frog quickly pulled the dough back out of the fire. She shed her frog skin, and once again Vasilisa the Wise ran to the window and clapped her hands to call her loyal maidens. "Be quick," she said. "I must have a cake such as the ones my father would have prepared for the grandest holidays."

Before morning the maidens returned with one of the most beautiful cakes ever seen. With its great gates and high domed roofs, it looked like a miniature city. Vasilisa placed the cake on a table by the sleeping Ivan, and slipped back into her frog skin.

The next morning, Ivan awoke and saw the magnificent cake. Carefully, he wrapped it and carried it to the Czar, who was receiving the cakes from his two elder sons.

Their wives had thrown the dough directly into the fire as their spy had reported, and their cakes were lopsided, black, and lumpy. When he tried to eat the first cake, the Czar almost broke a tooth it was so hard. Furious, he threw it on the floor! The second cake looked so dark and horrible, he didn't even bother to try it. He said, "I wouldn't want my dogs to eat this!"

But when the Czar saw Ivan's cake, he exclaimed with delight, "This cake is truly fit to grace the royal table!" and Ivan went home rejoicing.

It was not long, however, before the Czar summoned his sons to come to him for a third time. "Your wives have done all I've commanded," said the Czar. "Now I want you to bring them to my palace for a banquet."

The two older brothers went home to tell their wives, "At last, this frog bride must come to the palace for all to see!" Ivan, looking sadder than ever, returned home.

"Kwa, kwa," said his bride. "Why do you weep? Was your father not pleased with the cake?"

"Oh, yes, he was more than pleased," said the prince. "You have sewn the most handsome shirt, you have baked the most beautiful cake, but now you are to come with me to a

banquet at the palace. There everyone will see that you are just a lowly frog. I am ashamed to show you as my wife.''

''Do not grieve,'' said the frog. ''Go to bed, to sleep, and when you awake you will see the morning brings more wisdom than the evening.''

The next morning, the frog sent Ivan to the palace saying she would follow him in one hour. ''When you hear thunder,'' she said, ''you must tell the court that it's your frog bride arriving in her little carriage.''

So Prince Ivan went to the banquet alone, and when his brothers saw him they mocked: ''Where is your beautiful wife? You could have brought her in your handkerchief. You must have had to search every swamp in the kingdom to find such a wife!''

As they laughed, there was a sudden clap of thunder that made the whole palace shake. ''Do not be afraid, noble guests,'' said Ivan. ''That is my frog wife arriving in her little carriage.''

Everyone ran to the windows, where they saw a magnificent gold carriage drawn by six winged horses arrive at the palace gate.

Out of the coach stepped Vasilisa the Wise. She wore a blue silk gown that glittered with stars, and her long golden hair was crowned with a bright crescent moon. There were no words to convey her beauty. No one could take their eyes from her. She took her bewildered Ivan's arm, and he led her to the royal table.

The Czar was enchanted, and the wives of the two older princes watched her every movement. They were determined to do whatever she did.

They saw she did not drink all of her wine but rather poured the last remaining drops into her left sleeve. When she had finished eating the roast swan, she put the tiny bones into her right sleeve, and the other wives did the same.

After they had eaten their fill, the guests began to dance. Awed by the Frog Princess's grace and beauty, the Czar asked her to dance. As she danced gracefully over the floor, she waved her left arm and a beautiful lake appeared at one end of the banquet hall. She waved her right sleeve and a flock of seven swans swam upon that lake.

Then the wives of the two older princes tried the same thing. They waved their left sleeves, and all the guests were splashed with wine. They waved their right sleeves, and bones flew out—and one hit the Czar right in the eye. Outraged, he ordered them both out of the palace.

Meanwhile, Prince Ivan could not believe that his frog bride was really such a beautiful princess. Fearing she might turn back into a frog, he quickly left the palace for home to search for her frog skin. Once he found it, he threw it into the fire.

Vasilisa arrived at the house and when she did not find her frog skin she wept, "Oh, Prince Ivan, if only you could have been more patient! Now you have lost me forever, unless you can find me beyond three-times-nine lands in the thirtieth kingdom in the empire that lies under the sun, the realm of Old Bones the Immortal." Then Vasilisa the Wise turned into a blue dove and flew out the window.

Ivan wept for almost a year before the Czar gave him permission to search for his lost wife. He did not know where to begin, so he followed his eyes. Ivan walked for a long, long time. Many days had passed when he met a very old man, and he told him his story.

"Oh, Prince Ivan," the old man said, "why did you burn the frog skin? It was not yours to take. Vasilisa was born wiser than her own father, and in a jealous rage he turned her into a frog for three years. Her time was almost up, and if you had

not burned her frog skin, she would be with you now. I will give you this golden ball to help you find her. Throw it on the ground and follow it wherever it rolls.''

Ivan thanked the old man and followed the little gold ball as it led him across a plain and into a dense forest. Then, in a small clearing, it stopped before a bear. Ivan drew his bow and was just about to shoot when the bear spoke to him. ''Don't kill me, Prince Ivan, for one day I will be able to help you.''

Ivan put down his bow and continued on his way. Before long, he spotted a drake flying overhead. He was about to shoot it when the duck cried out, ''Do not kill me, Prince Ivan, for one day I will help you.'' The prince spared the drake and went on.

Suddenly, a hare ran across his path. As Ivan was about to shoot it, it too cried out, ''Don't kill me, Prince Ivan, for one day I will be able to help you.'' Again, Ivan put down his bow and continued on his way after the rolling ball.

Next, he came upon a pike lying on the shore beside a beautiful lake. The fish, gasping for breath, asked Ivan to please help him back into the lake. Ivan took pity on the poor fish, threw it back into the lake, and walked on.

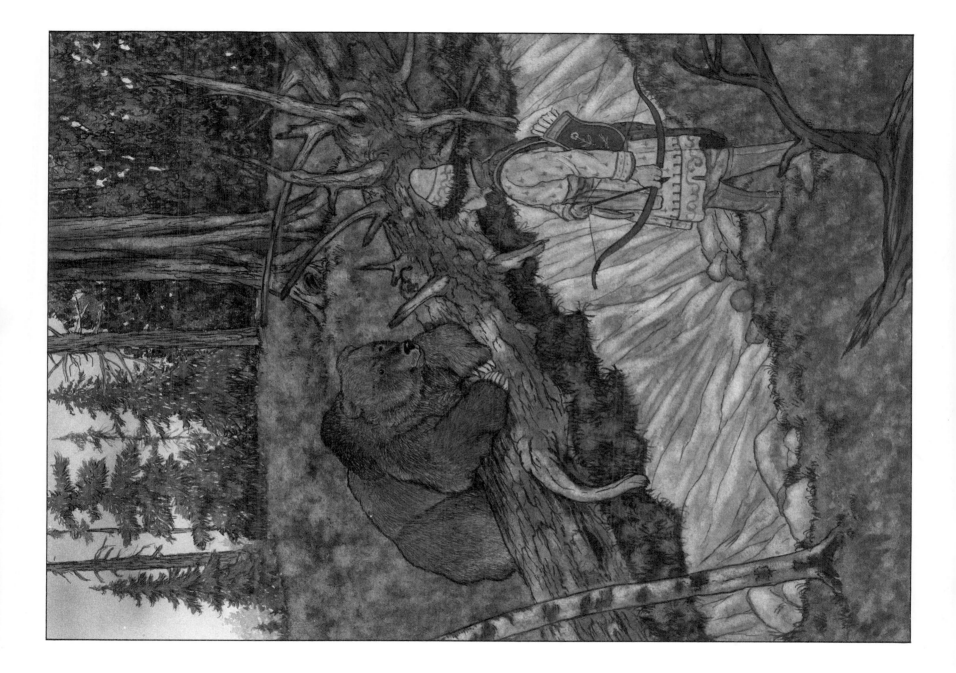

Much later, the golden ball stopped before a hut in the forest. It was a strange house built on chicken legs, and it turned round and round continually. Ivan commanded:

"Little hut, little hut,
Stand the way thy Mother placed thee,
With thy back to the wood and thy front to me!"

At once the hut stood still.

Ivan climbed up one of the chicken legs and opened the door. Inside he saw the oldest of the Baba Yagas, the grand-mother of all the witches. She was sitting on top of a stove, her bony old hands curled around a wooden cane.

"What brings you here?" she screeched at Ivan.

"Is that any way to greet a great Russian?" said the Prince. "I have traveled long and far, and I am very hungry. First, heat up a bath and prepare some food for me, and then I'll tell you my story."

The Baba Yaga was delighted with his spirit, so she pre-pared a bath and some food for him. Once he had refreshed himself, he told her his sad story.

"Yes, I know where you can find her," said the Baba Yaga. "She's in the hands of the evil Koshchey, Old Bones the Immortal. It will be very difficult to rescue her because no one has been able to slay Old Koshchey. His death is at the end of a needle, the needle is in an egg, which is inside a duck. The duck is in the belly of a hare, and the hare is inside a chest on top of a tall oak tree that Koshchey guards."

The Baba Yaga told Ivan how to get to the sturdy oak tree. Toward evening, he found it and saw the chest nestled in the very top branches, safely beyond anyone's reach.

He waited until he knew Old Koshchey was asleep and tried to shake the chest down, but it wouldn't budge. Frustrated, the Prince sat down.

Suddenly, from out of nowhere, came the bear. With one powerful blow from his paw, he uprooted the tree, and the chest came crashing to the ground. It split open, and out hopped a rabbit, who scurried into the forest. Just as it took off, the hare appeared. It ran after the rabbit, caught it, and tore it to pieces.

A duck flew out of the belly of the dead rabbit. Immediately, the drake appeared in the sky and swooped down on the flying duck with such force that the frightened duck dropped an egg, which fell right into the middle of the lake.

You can imagine Ivan's despair, as he thought he would never be able to retrieve that egg from the bottom of the lake. Just when Ivan had given up hope, he saw the pike swimming toward the shore. And in its mouth was the egg.

Ivan took the egg and cracked it open and found the needle. Slowly, he bent the needle back and forth, and as he did so the sleeping Old Koshchey began to sway back and forth in agony.

Finally, Ivan broke off the tip of the needle, and that was the end of Old Bones the Immortal.

Ivan rushed inside Old Koshchey's black palace and found Vasilisa the Wise. She threw herself into his arms and exclaimed, "Now I can be with you forever!"

Then the Baba Yaga gave them a beautiful white horse that could fly like the wind. In four days it carried Ivan and his bride Vasilisa back to the Czar's palace. The Czar rejoiced to have them home and gave a great feast in their honor, and on the evening of the feast he announced that Ivan would succeed him as Czar of all the Russias.